BANNED DRABBLES

Compiled & Edited by
Ben Thomas & D Kershaw

**Also available and coming soon
from Black Hare Press**

DARK DRABBLES SERIES
WORLDS
ANGELS
MONSTERS
BEYOND
UNRAVEL
APOCALYPSE
LOVE
HATE
OCEANS
ANCIENTS

SPECIAL EDITIONS
STORMING AREA 51
EERIE CHRISTMAS
BAD ROMANCE
TWENTY TWENTY
SCHOOL'S IN

OTHERS
DEEP SPACE
WHAT IF?
KEY TO THE KINGDOM
DEEP SEA
BEYOND THE REALM
BANNED
WETWARE

Twitter: @BlackHarePress
Facebook: BlackHarePress
Website: www.BlackHarePress.com

TABLE OF CONTENTS

BANNED DRABBLES

FOREWORD
DEAN KERSHAW

Horror is highly subjective—what one person fears isn't necessarily mirrored by everyone else. For instance, some people think spiders are cute—despite their many hairy legs; numerous obsidian pools that watch your every move while they calculate just the right moment to pounce; enzyme-injecting fangs that liquidise you so they can digest you easier...uhm...I mean, their food easier...

Some people even keep spiders as pets (shudders)! I'd burn down the house, the car, the neighbourhood, the refuse collection truck that came that morning, just to be rid of the terror-inducing monsters!

Earlier this year, we set a challenge for our authors to come up with horror-themed stories using a song title of their own choice as a prompt—zombies, vampyres, killer spiders, etc...

And, boy, did their dark little minds come up

with some blood-thirsty, twisted, heavy metal tales.

We did something a little different with this anthology. This publication is a prelude—a taster, if you will—to the main stories you'll find in the main *Banned*. We hope—nay, guarantee—you'll enjoy them as much as we did.

Love and kisses

Dean Kershaw

Editor-in-Chief
BLACK HARE PRESS

FRACTURED FAIRYTALE
ALANNA ROBERTSON-WEBB

If you saw Elise and Courtney, you would think they were the best of friends, just a normal pair of siren and pixie teens practising their band's song set as they navigated the choppy waters of high school. Smiles and laughter were what their classmates saw, but underneath that illusion of happiness was festering anger.

Elise has used Courtney as a doormat for too long, and with a monstrous secret looming between them, tension is mounting. With a month until their first show, is there any hope for these two to reconcile in time?

Things are about to get *electrifying*.

BLACK HARE PRESS

TRANSMISSION
ANTONIA RACHEL WARD

15th January: On this day in 1980, Sid Rockwell, the enigmatic lead singer of post-punk band Atrocity Exhibition, walked out of a gig at Newcastle City Hall and was last spotted heading towards the Tyne Bridge. A report from the band's manager, Nigel Chatham, suggested that Rockwell had been suffering from blackouts in the days leading up to his disappearance. No evidence ever came to light to explain what had happened to him, and twenty-five years later, the case remains unsolved. Atrocity Exhibition went on to have several top ten hits without Rockwell, including their only number one single, "Transmission."

POWERSLAVE
BETH W. PATTERSON

Chivalry is a very good thing, often tied to good manners and common sense. But anything foisted upon another person is inexcusable. Don't let looks deceive you. The slender young woman carrying her own equipment knows what she's doing. She knows how to lift with her legs, not her back. She's stronger than she appears. Oh yes, and she might really be an immortal being. This is heavy metal after all.

Never touch someone's equipment, specifically when told not to. And don't ever interfere with performances. But the number one crime in the music industry is underestimating a person.

BLACK HARE PRESS

PIECE OF MY HEART
CHRIS BANNOR

"It's only while he plays, right?" his Mama asked.

"Of course."

Columbus hid behind her legs, but the stranger bent his knees and grinned at him. His smile was pretty, but it reminded him of the guy that used to sleep in his mom's bed and gave him a bloody lip and made him lie to his Mama about it.

"Just say yes," the odd man said, teeth gleaming ivory, like dog fangs.

"Come on, baby. Mama needs this one thing of you."

"Yes." But Mama had that gleam in her eyes, and he knew he'd just done something bad.

FROM HER TO ETERNITY

DAVID GREEN

"Katherine, you've got to go. Long day of recording tomorrow."

Her lips brush against my neck, fingers tracing my chest and down my abdomen. I met Katherine at a bar earlier tonight. She's intoxicating.

"It can wait, Nick," she whispers, "aren't the vocals done last?"

I try to answer but the words disappear when her hand reaches my crotch. Katherine nibbles at my neck.

"You worry too much," she murmurs, "let me help."

I close my eyes and surrender. The nibble at my neck turns to a pleasurable pain as her teeth pierce my skin, and I slide into darkness.

BLACK HARE PRESS

JUST A SINGER IN A ROCK N ROLL BAND
GREGG CUNNINGHAM

Wantham is a cesspit for all things evil. The backstreet nightclubs are squeezed by underworld scum like Russian kingpin Vanivich and his thugs out to make a fast buck without any regard for those beneath them, throttling livelihoods until businesses comply.

Dirty cops, under orders from mob bosses, cascade their misery on, spreading intimidation to nightclub owners offering protection for favours. Struggling artists, like Dmitri Timbrado, flip burgers part time while they peddle the mobs Dexi dime bags to the street rats out to get a hit from whatever *Heisenburger* catering truck offers.

Some might say isn't life strange.

WHILE MY GUITAR GENTLY WEEPS
HOLLEY CORNETTO

"Dude, I fuckin' sold my soul. Know what it got me? Nothin'." Jason collapsed onto the couch.

"Not nothin'." Kelly sat beside him. "You shred guitar like it's fuckin' Wheaties, man."

"I wanted to be the best guitarist since Slash. What I didn't say was 'I wanna be famous' or 'I wanna go platinum'. And you know why? Because my stupid ass thought being good was good enough."

He reached for the closest bottle of Heineken, sniffed, and downed it.

"You know what we need?" Kelly said, kicking a Cheetos bag across the floor. "We need an epic fucking song."

BLACK HARE PRESS

SAY YOU LOVE ME OR SAY GOODNIGHT

J.W. GARRETT

CeCe shoved her guitar and two suitcases into the trunk. "Ready?" the driver asked. Glancing at her childhood home, she blinked back tears. *Someday you'll be proud. You'll see. Maybe I can even make up for the grief I caused.*

The fence latch screeched as she shoved it closed. She lingered a few seconds longer, staring inside her bedroom window where her dreams had been born—where music had lived day and night. The one constant in her life. Her parents had died because of her…hating her. Now it was time to change that. Show them what she'd become.

ANGIE BABY

KIMBERLY REI

It was the worst date ever. Not that she'd been on many. Seventeen and her father still loomed over her. But he was working late, and she'd had a crush on Jake for years.

Now Jake was in her room, all hands and tongue. Calling this a mistake would be a kindness.

She pushed Jake's hand away and reached for the stereo, lowering the volume. She wanted him to leave. She glanced back, and a warm tingle slid over her skin. Jake was fading away. As the music drifted to nothing, so did he.

She shivered, grinning. She felt…satisfied.

WHO WANTS TO LIVE FOREVER

MAXINE CHURCHMAN

"Mummy! Look at this." Betty pressed her nose against the cool glass for a better look at the miniature ballerina, poised ready to start dancing. "She looks so real."

"Incredible! Look at her eyes and fingernails," agreed her mother.

Betty pointed to a coin slot. "Can we watch her dance?"

The ballerina leaped and twirled around the confines of the diorama to a haunting melody. Entranced, Betty marvelled at how the ballerina could move so realistically with no visible means of the maker's mechanism, and how, when the music stopped, there was a perfect tear on the ballerina's cheek.

THE LAST DRINK
MELINDA POUNCEY

Jimmy watched on the backstage monitors as the arena began to fill up. The tour was going well, but he was already bored with the groupies and hangers on. He was craving something different. His manager was usually pretty good about supplying him with what he needed but, of course, had to have something to work with, and the jaded fans had become as jaded as he through the years, perhaps picking up on his cynicism through his music. All Jimmy knew is that he needed a change, and soon, or the whole tour would be a bust.

Maybe tonight…

CROSS ROAD BLUES
RAVEN CORINN CARLUK

At the crossroad
Five black candles
Right at midnight

At the crossroad
Black robe chanting
Call our Master

Come, we all wait. Come, seal our fate.
Rise up from Hell, we've something to sell
Accept our sacrifice

At the crossroad
Light the fires
Burn the body

At the crossroad
Drinking hot blood
Untie the virgin

We hear your voice. Worship you by choice.
Our lives are yours. Your power we implore.
Praise His Majesty

At the crossroad
Seal the bargain
Right at midnight

At the crossroad
Fame and fortune
Hail the Master

Accept our sacrifice. Praise His Majesty.
The crossroad

THE NIGHT CREEPER
ROBIN BRAID

Skilled rock guitarist required to join kickass three piece with smarts, presence, and a rockin' van. We're embarking on a journey to the beyond and back, and we want YOU along for the ride. Influences unimportant but must be open minded and ready to crush the whole damn world and cleanse it with hellfire. Take the trip, turn from the light, and embrace the beauty that lays in darkness. Offer us your soul, and your nightmares will become dreams. No timewasters, prima donnas or poseurs, and absolutely no wankers.

Call the Night Creeper on 07700 900666.

WAITING FOR THE BEGINNING

STEVEN STREETER

Talent.

It was something that he thought he had. Believing that, he had tried so hard to make it in the world he had adored since he had been a child. He had been encouraged by well-meaning family and friends, but what if they had all lied to him?

What if he did not have talent?

To get up on stage and sing for an audience.

All he had ever wanted.

There was one thing for it. Just one thing.

A deal with the Devil.

It had worked for Robert Johnson. It would work for him.

What could go wrong?

SEX TYPE THING

S.O. GREEN

Lisa-Marie Kenyon was gone. The mousey-haired, doe-eyed, rabbit-toothed girl had transformed into a wolf.

Her name was Jezebel. Her band was Sin. So was her lifestyle.

They asked her the secret of their popularity. She said, "Me."

They asked her if she ever lip-synched. She said, "Only if I meet a girl I really like."

They asked her about the suicides. The bloody knives, the swinging ropes, the empty bleach bottles. She said, "It's beautiful, isn't it? To inspire so much passion."

"Isn't that kind of talk irresponsible?" they asked her.

"I believe in individual freewill," she said, "don't you?"

NIGHTMARES MADE FLESH

SAM M. PHILLIPS

I woke up to a terrible burden being placed upon my soul, and yet I didn't know it. There was a hunger, and it was just opening, like a flower full of ravenous, biting teeth, blooming into consciousness, ready to feed.

I wasn't sure if I was prey or not.

The window blew closed, and with it, my mind snapped shut and I couldn't see anymore; all the light in my life had been snuffed out. Feeling sorry for myself wasn't going to achieve anything, so I got up, looked at my phone.

It was the day of the gig.

BLACK HARE PRESS

TORN
STACEY JAINE MCINTOSH

A girl is shackled to the concrete wall, cuffed with cold iron that bites into her skin.

Tears prick her eyes, but she refuses to cry.

"This is punishment for your crimes committed against the Winter Court."

In one fluid motion, the executioner tears her fragile wings from her shoulder blades, leaving her broken and bleeding. Rivulets of blood cascade down her back, turning her milky white skin crimson.

Keys jangle, bringing her out of her pain fuelled daze, and back into the present—back to the smoke-filled nightclub with its live cover band.

"Ferelith!" the band's drummer Atticus shouts.

THE MAN WHO SOLD THE WORLD

STEPHANIE SCISSOM

On my twenty-fifth birthday, I inherited 490 million dollars from my rockstar father's estate. The next day, I spent it all to bring him back.

Because of the exorbitant cost, "resurrections" were out of reach for most, and because of public frenzy, most of the ones who did buy them didn't talk about them.

So, I went into it blind, but I didn't care. I'd lost my dad when I was six, and my heart's desire was to have him back. I'd braced myself for anything.

Anything except for the fact that his suicide hadn't been a suicide at all.

TEENAGERS
STEPHEN HERCZEG

Growing old seems wrong to me
Remaining young is where I'll be
Can you help me find the key?
Bring that teenage blood to me

Sometimes I can't stand my face
You'll not see me in this place
Break all the mirrors just in case
Teenage blood I long to taste

I hate the lines time has wrought
All my riches led to nought
Against my death I've always fought
Seek teenage blood the lesson taught

Their succour smooths out my skin
God botherers call it sin
For millennia, it's how I've been
Bathed in blood is how I win

BLACK HARE PRESS

BODY ELECTRIC
TIM MENDEES

Drip! Drip! Drip!

Blood splashed onto the plastic cassette box. Dan wiped his nose with the back of his hand. He cursed and wiped the case down his denims.

Clicking the tape off and removing the headphones, he slipped the offensive recording back into its box and shuddered.

Something about the music, if you could call it music, made his head feel funny. The relentless drone, punishing metallic beats, and agonised howling seriously affected his equilibrium. His vision had blurred, and his blood fizzed in his veins. He couldn't handle it…

But he knew a couple of dudes who could…

BLACK HARE PRESS

HERE COMES MY GIRL
TRISHA MCKEE

Susie did as they asked and left everything behind.

They ushered her to a secluded cabin and put her through training. Voice and dance, the history of the band, the way to answer questions during an interview.

But the true test came when a lady arrived with herbs in her hand and chants on her tongue. The true test came when Susie was no longer Susie. They placed that guitar in her hands, and she played with the fire of a true talent, of a soul thought to be long gone. She played as if her life depended on it.

WHORE
ZOEY XOLTON

"Darling," croons the succubus.

"Yes, Lilith?"

"I'm bored."

"Bored? How can you be? There's more cock in Hell than anywhere else in the Verse."

Lilith crawls onto the Fallen Angel's lap. "I crave an adventure," she pouts.

Lucifer sighs. "You're incorrigible."

"That's why you love me, my king," she whispers into his ear.

Lucifer's silver-blue eyes gleam as he smiles. "Just one of the many reasons," he concedes. "And you know that I can't say '*no*' to you."

Lilith bites her lip, pleading.

"As you wish," he grants. "How do you feel about putting your siren song to good use?"

BLACK HARE PRESS

ABOUT THE PUBLISHER

BLACK HARE PRESS is a small, independent publisher based in Melbourne, Australia.

Founded in 2018, our aim has always been to champion emerging authors from all around the globe and offer opportunities for them to participate in speculative fiction and horror short story anthologies.

www.blackharepress.com

www.ingramcontent.com/pod-product-compliance
Lightning Source LLC
Chambersburg PA
CBHW031036190726
48286CB00003BA/1200